# The Case of the Chocolate Fingerprints

Look for these Clue™ Jr. books!

# The Case of the Chocolate Fingerprints

Book created by Parker C. Hinter

Written by Della Rowland

Illustrated by Sam Viviano

Based on characters from the Parker Brothers game

A Creative Media Applications Production

SCHOLASTIC INC.
New York Toronto London Auckland Sydney

ISBN 0-590-26217-3

12 11 10 9 8 7 6 5 4 3 2          5 6 7 8 9/9 0/0

Printed in the U.S.A.                    40

First Scholastic printing, July 1995

# Contents

# Contents

# The Case of the Chocolate Fingerprints

# Introduction

Meet the members of the Clue Club.

Samantha Scarlet, Peter Plum, Georgie Green, Wendy White, Mortimer Mustard, and Polly Peacock.

These young detectives are all in the same fourth-grade class. The thing they have most in common, though, is their love of mysteries. They formed the Clue Club to talk about mystery books they have read, mystery TV shows and movies they like to watch, and also, to play their favorite game, Clue Jr.

These mystery fans are pretty sharp when it comes to solving real-life mysteries, too. They all use their wit and deductive skills to crack the cases in this book.

You can match *your* wits with this gang of junior detectives to solve the eight mysteries. Can you guess who did it? Check the solution that appears upside down after the story to see if you were right!

# The Case of the Forgotten Day

Everyone in the Clue Club stood outside the rug store. Everyone, that is, except Peter Plum. Polly Peacock, Mortimer Mustard, Samantha Scarlet, Wendy White, and Georgie Green looked up and down the street. "Peter is always late," sighed Mortimer.

It was Memorial Day weekend. Every year the rug store changed into the town flea market on Memorial Day. The owners rolled up all the carpets and moved the rugs so that people could set up tables inside. This year, kids were allowed to have their own tables. The Clue Club was eager to see what the other children might be selling, so they had decided to get there early. But they were waiting for Peter.

3

Finally, they saw him running down the block.

"Here I am," puffed Peter.

"Late as usual, Peter," Polly said sternly. "Let's get a look at the tables before all the good things are gone."

As the kids walked into the rug store, Wendy asked, "So, Peter, where were you?"

"I went to school," Peter said, blushing. "I forgot it was Memorial Day and school is closed."

"Peter! It's a national holiday. Everything is closed," laughed Samantha.

"How could you forget to remember Memorial Day?" Georgie giggled. "Especially when you get a day off from school!"

"Exactly," said Mortimer. "Memorial Day reminds us that soon school will be out for good! Or at least for a good summer."

"I'm giving a report, and I guess I was really looking forward to it," Peter said. He started to tell them about it.

"Look over there!" interrupted Wendy.

"Gregory Grape has a booth! Let's see what he's selling."

Gregory was in their fourth-grade class. He had carefully placed a few items on a small table. He showed the kids a pair of outgrown Rollerblades, space hero T-shirts, baseball cards, and some jewelry.

"How much is that pearl necklace?" Polly asked.

"It's two dollars," said Gregory.

"That's too much, Gregory," Polly told him. "I won't have enough money left for other things."

"I think so, too," Gregory said. "But the necklace isn't mine. I owe my sister a favor. I told her I would sell some of her old jewelry. She said I couldn't change any of the prices even one penny. She thinks I'm an idiot."

"I'll come back if I have enough money left," said Polly.

The kids visited other tables. Peter bought some old mystery books for a dime apiece from the library's table. Polly picked up a scarf that was green and purple and gold, and a yard long. "This is only fifty cents," she cried. "Now that's a flea market price."

Georgie found a baseball with Don Mattingly's picture and autograph on it. "I can't believe anyone would sell this!" he exclaimed.

Samantha got a T-shirt with a cat on it. Wendy bought some barrettes and a tiny mirror for Petunia, her parrot. Mortimer bought some new sunglasses from a booth that Best-View, the glasses store, had set up. "I don't like old things," he said.

The flea market closed at three o'clock. Around two-thirty, people began packing up their sale items. The Clue Club had seen everything and they were ready to leave. On their way out, the kids passed Gregory's table again. Gregory was upset.

"What's wrong, Gregory?" asked Georgie.

"That pearl necklace Polly liked is missing," Gregory sighed. "And my sister will expect me to give her the two dollars. I told her that was too much and she'd never sell it. Now someone stole it and I'll have to pay her the full price. I'll be so glad when she goes off to college!"

The kids helped Gregory look for the necklace on the floor around his table, but it was nowhere to be found.

"I've got a quarter you can have toward the two dollars," said Polly.

"Here's thirty cents," said Georgie.

Altogether the kids pitched in a dollar and twenty-five cents. "Thanks, guys. You've made living with my sister a lot less painful," Gregory told them.

The next day on the school playground the kids heard Gregory yelling at Vicki Gold. Vicki was wearing a necklace that looked exactly like the one Gregory was selling.

"You stole that necklace from my booth yesterday!" Gregory shouted. "You were looking at it all morning. You got mad when I told you I couldn't sell it for less than two dollars."

"It wasn't worth two dollars and you know it," Vicki said. "But I didn't steal it. I got this necklace at another table. There are millions of pearl necklaces in the world, you know. Besides I left the flea market at noon."

"The necklace was there when I looked at it around two o'clock," Polly reminded Gregory.

"I thought I saw you there later, Vicki," Samantha said. "It was right before the tables closed at three o'clock."

"Impossible," said Vicki. "I was at the bank with my mother. We were there from two-thirty until it closed at three o'clock. We were opening a savings account for me. There's no way I could be in two places at once."

"And there's no way you could have been at the bank," said Peter. "You're lying, Vicki."

**How did Peter know Vicki was lying about being at the bank?**

# Solution
# The Case of the Forgotten Day

"How do you know Vicki wasn't at the bank?" asked Gregory.

"Yesterday was Memorial Day," Peter said. "It's a national holiday, and all the banks are closed. So Vicki is lying about being there."

"Okay, Gregory," said Vicki, pouting. "I'll give you your stupid two dollars for the necklace."

"No, you won't," said Gregory. "You'll give the necklace to Polly. She wanted it, too. She and the others gave me most of the money to pay my sister. Plus they found the thief. That deserves a reward."

"At least you remembered the banks are closed on Memorial Day," Georgie said, laughing at Peter. "Maybe next year you'll remember that school is closed, too."

# The Case of the Chocolate Fingerprints

The Clue Club was having its annual summer Clue Jr. tournament. The games were supposed to begin at ten o'clock that morning in the park. Mortimer Mustard and Georgie Green were on their way there to help set up tables.

"Today is supposed to be the hottest day of the whole summer," said Mortimer. He wiped his face with his shirtsleeve.

"We're lucky the park let us use the snack bar for our tournament," said Georgie. "It's air-conditioned."

When the boys arrived at the snack bar, Wendy White, Samantha Scarlet, and Polly Peacock were already there. They were busy putting the Clue Jr. games out on the tables.

"Ah," sighed Mortimer, dropping his backpack on the floor. "Cool air!"

"Oh, good. You're here," said Wendy. "Could you grab some chairs? They're over there against the wall."

Peter Plum was helping Mr. Plaid, who ran the snack bar. Mr. Plaid was getting the food and drinks ready. He took some chocolate bars out of the refrigerator and arranged them in the racks on the counter.

"You keep candy in the refrigerator?" asked Peter.

"The park turns off the air-conditioning in here at night," said Mr. Plaid. "When it's this hot, I keep my chocolate bars in the refrigerator. Otherwise, they'll melt."

By ten o'clock the other players were all there. The Clue Club kids formed three groups. Peter and Wendy led one group. Mortimer and Polly were in charge of another. And Georgie and Samantha headed up the third. By eleven-thirty, after several good games, the players decided to break for lunch. Most of them lined up at the snack bar counter for pizza, hamburgers, hot dogs, and fries.

"I have to run home and check on Bizzy," Peter told the group. "It's so hot, I want to make sure he has plenty of water. Sometimes he knocks his water bowl over."

"I'm going home to eat," said Nora Navy. "I want a tuna fish sandwich."

"I want to eat at home, too," said Paul Peach.

"Me, too," said Hunter Brown. "My favorite TV show comes on at noon."

As the four kids left, Samantha called out, "We'll start the second round of games at twelve-thirty." But at twelve-thirty Nora, Paul, Hunter, and Peter still weren't back from lunch.

"Peter is always late," Polly said to Mortimer, shaking her head.

Just then Peter came in the door and ran over to his table. "Sorry to be late," he said. "I was reading about how they make chocolate while I ate lunch. I guess I forgot about the time. Is everyone here?"

"Everyone in our group is here," Samantha said to Georgie.

"Nora and Hunter aren't back yet," Wendy told Peter.

"We'll have to wait for them," shrugged Peter. "That's half our group."

"Paul's not back, either," said Polly. "And he's on my team."

"I guess we have to wait," said Mortimer. "Oh, well, they'll be here soon. So tell us how they make chocolate, Peter."

Before Peter could even start talking, Nora ran in the door. "Sorry, guys," she said. "Mom asked me to water her roses just as I was leaving."

Hunter showed up next. "I know I'm late, but it's too hot to run!" he panted. "So it took me longer to get back after my show."

Paul was right behind Hunter. "I'm here, too," he called. "Let's play Clue Jr."

"Okay!" shouted Georgie. "Everyone is here. Time for round two!"

Everyone sat down and began a new

game. Suddenly Hunter stood up. "I have to have a soda," he said. "Walking in this heat made me really thirsty."

"I know what you mean," agreed Nora. "Walking home made me so thirsty I had three glasses of lemonade for lunch."

"Why don't we all get drinks," said Samantha. "Then maybe we can get on with the game."

Everyone lined up at the snack bar counter again. As Polly got up to join the others, she noticed dirty fingerprints on her game. "Look at this! Someone must have eaten mud pies for lunch!" she cried. "Can everybody wipe off their hands? We don't want our games ruined."

The kids returned to the games with clean hands, and the tournament continued. After about half an hour, Mr. Plaid came over to Peter and asked if he could talk to the Clue Club. They followed him over to the snack bar counter.

"I hate to tell you this, but a whole box of Chock-O-Late bars is missing," Mr.

Plaid told the kids. "I took the box out of the refrigerator this morning and put it on the counter by the door. I was going to put some of the bars in the candy rack. Then I decided to put more drinks in the refrigerator. I didn't notice it was gone until after lunch."

"The only people who have been in the snack bar are kids playing Clue Jr.," said Samantha. "It has to be someone in the tournament."

"Oh, how awful!" cried Wendy. "We have to solve this crime or the park might not let us have our tournament here anymore."

"Wait a minute," said Peter. "When I came back from lunch I saw some Chock-O-Late wrappers outside the snack bar door. Let's see if they lead us anywhere."

"Listen, guys," Mortimer called out to the other players. "Keep playing. We'll be back soon."

The kids followed the trail of candy wrappers to the nearby toddler playground. The swings and slides and seesaws were in the shapes of animals. The swings were suspended between two giant squirrels. The slide went down an elephant's trunk, and the sandbox sat on a beaver's broad, flat tail.

"Look back here," called Wendy, pointing beside the slide. The kids spotted a pile of Chock-O-Late wrappers and the empty candy box.

"Here's another crime," said Mortimer, picking up a wrapper. "Littering."

Mortimer threw the wrapper in a trash can. "Now I have melted chocolate all over my hand," he complained.

"We've found the candy, but how can we tell who took it?" asked Georgie.

"Well, it had to be someone who left the snack bar at lunchtime," said Peter. "That was me, Nora, Hunter, and Paul."

"Well, we know it wasn't you," said Samantha. Then she laughed. "Or was it?"

"Very funny, Samantha," said Peter.

"Hey, look," said Georgie, pointing

to the side of the slide. "There are choco-late fingerprints all over the slide. It's so hot the chocolate must have melted in the thief's hand."

"That still doesn't tell us who took the candy," said Samantha.

"Let's go back to the tournament," said Peter. "Maybe we'll come up with some-thing on the way."

When they got to the snack bar, the kids noticed more fingerprints on the outside of the door.

"Hey, more chocolate fingerprints," said Wendy.

"I didn't notice those when I came in," said Peter.

"I know who the chocolate culprit is," said Mortimer, snapping his fingers. "Let's go in. I want to do this like Hercule Poirot does in the Agatha Christie stories. First he gets all the suspects together. Then he explains to everybody how the crime hap-pened and who the thief is."

Mortimer stopped the games and told

the other players about the stolen candy.

"Whoever took a box of Chock-O-Late bars from Mr. Plaid's snack bar left fingerprints everywhere," said Mortimer. "Chocolate fingerprints. First he left fingerprints on the slide where the candy was eaten. Then he left fingerprints on the door when he came into the snack bar after lunch."

"So, who is it, Hercule Mustard?" asked Georgie.

**Can you guess who stole the chocolate?**

# Solution
## The Case of the Chocolate Fingerprints

"It's Paul," said Mortimer.

"Me?" cried Paul. "But Peter or Nora or Hunter could have left those fingerprints on the door."

"True, but you also left chocolate fingerprints someplace else," said Mortimer. "On Polly's game. Polly thought they were mud. But they were chocolate."

"But how do you know it was me?" asked Paul.

"There were four people who left the snack bar," explained Mortimer. "You were the only one on Polly's team. So, you're the only one who could have left fingerprints on her game."

"Mortimer's right. I took the candy," Paul admitted. "But I promise I'll pay you back, Mr. Plaid."

"Some Clue Jr. player you are, Paul," said Georgie. "You got caught because you left your fingerprints everywhere."

# 3

# The Case of Lost Time

It was Saturday morning. This was the day the Clue Club usually had its weekly meeting. Bright and early that morning, Georgie Green called Mortimer Mustard. "Mortimer," Georgie said, "how about we have our meeting at Mama Sophie's Pizza Parlor?"

"Fabulous idea, Georgie," exclaimed Mortimer. "Let's call the others."

So Georgie called Samantha Scarlet and Polly Peacock, and Mortimer called Peter Plum and Wendy White. By lunchtime, the Clue Club was busy eating and playing.

After an hour or so, Wendy leaned back in her chair and stretched. "I lose track of time when we play Clue Jr. What time is it, Georgie?" she asked.

"Don't know," Georgie replied. "I can't find my new watch. I was helping Mom weed the garden in the backyard yesterday. I took off the watch and hung it on the fence before I watered the tomatoes. When I went to get it after lunch, the watch was gone."

Just then Richie Royal, the town bully, came into the pizza parlor. He made his way through the crowded parlor to the counter. As he walked past the Clue Club's table, he bumped Wendy's chair.

"Oh, excuse me!" he said, and bowed low in front of Wendy. "I didn't see you. You're so small, you're hard to see, you know." Then he laughed, and Wendy looked down at the ground.

"And bullies are easy to spot," said Georgie. "They always make themselves stand out."

Richie sneered at the kids and moved on up to the counter, bumping a few more chairs.

"That looks like your watch," Mortimer said to Georgie. He pointed to the watch Richie was wearing.

"It *is* my watch," exclaimed Georgie. "Hey, Richie!" he called out. "What are you doing with my watch?"

"What are you talking about?" Richie said. "I come in to get a simple slice and get accused of something right away."

Mama Sophie came out from behind the counter. "What's the problem, kids?" she said.

"That's my watch," Georgie repeated.

"I found this watch by the side of my house," shrugged Richie. "It can't be yours. You've never even been to my house."

"You know that's my watch," said Georgie, shaking his head.

"Yeah? How do I know it's your watch?" asked Richie.

"Because you've been trying to get it away from me for a week," said Georgie. "The other day you tried to get me to sell

it to you. Then you tried to win it from me with some weird bet."

"So. That was a week ago. I wasn't near your house yesterday," Richie said.

"I know that's my watch!" shouted Georgie.

"Boys! Boys!" said Mama. "We can't have a fight in here."

"You can't prove this is your watch," grinned Richie. "There are plenty of watches like this one."

"He might be right, Georgie," said Mama. "Can you prove it's your watch?"

"I guess not," Georgie sighed.

"That's right, Clue Punk," Richie laughed.

"Wrong, Clue Klutz," said Samantha angrily. "And I have just the clue to prove it."

**How did Samantha know the watch belonged to Georgie?**

# Solution
# The Case of Lost Time

"You took Georgie's watch," Samantha said to Richie.

"How do you know?" asked Mama.

"Yeah," sneered Richie. "Rave on, sister."

"No one said the watch was taken yesterday," said Samantha. "If you know that, then you must be the one who took it."

"She's got a good point," said Mama. "I think we should call the policeman outside to come in and take care of things from here."

"Nah," said Richie, taking off the watch. "I was only kidding. Here's your time-piece, punk. Next time don't leave it hanging around. You could lose time that way. Heh, heh."

"Yeah, Richie," said Polly. "And if you don't stop taking things that aren't yours, someday you might be *doing* time."

Georgie put his watch on. "I think we've found some more time to play Clue Jr. How about it, Clue Club?"

# The Case of the Parrot's Escape

The weather was so warm, the Clue Club decided to have a picnic in Wendy White's backyard. Peter Plum brought his own special potato salad. Samantha Scarlet baked brownies. Polly Peacock wasn't much of a cook, so she brought cold cuts. And Georgie Green made fresh lemonade. Mortimer Mustard brought three different kinds of pickles and olives and some tapes of old radio shows that belonged to his father.

"This one is called *The Shadow*," said Mortimer. "Dad has a big collection of old radio shows. His favorites are the mysteries. That's probably why I'm so crazy about mysteries."

"It's not fair to blame your father for being crazy," Georgie said.

"So-o-o funny," droned Mortimer. "Anyway, the tapes got packed away when we moved to our new house. Dad just found a couple of boxes of them in the attic. They're really great!"

Mortimer put a tape into the tape recorder. "The best way to listen to a radio show is to sit back and close your eyes," he told his friends.

All of the kids stretched out on the grass or curled up in a lawn chair and closed their eyes. When the tape ended, they opened their eyes and began talking about the show.

"You were right about closing your eyes, Mortimer," said Peter.

"Yeah," exclaimed Samantha. "I could see everything that was happening in my mind."

"I didn't know I could hear so well!" laughed Georgie.

"One thing I kept hearing was Mr. White whistling," said Polly. She looked over at

Mr. White, who was washing the windows and whistling merrily.

"Your dad acts like he loves to wash windows, Wendy," said Peter.

"It's his spring thing," said Wendy, shaking her head. "Every spring he washes the windows inside and out. It's his way of welcoming the new season. He always starts at the top of the house and works his way down." She laughed. "And he always whistles the whole time."

"Wendy, look!" cried Samantha, pointing up. "There's Petunia." The kids looked up to see Wendy's pet parrot, Petunia, in the tree branches above their heads.

"How'd she get out?" said Wendy. "Petunia! Petunia! Come down to me!"

After a couple of minutes of calling, Petunia finally flew down to Wendy.

"I let her fly loose in the house to get some exercise," said Wendy. "I guess she got out when one of us came through the door. I'll be right back." She carried Petunia back inside the house.

Wendy came back with paper plates, cups, and plastic forks. The group began eating lunch. After a few bites, Georgie got up. "I need some more napkins," he said, walking into the house.

When he came out carrying a handful of napkins, Mortimer had another tape ready. "This one is called *The Whistler*," Mortimer said, "in honor of your father, Wendy."

All of a sudden the kids heard Petunia singing "Happy Birthday." She sang the song seven times before she would fly down to Wendy.

"Can't you teach her a few more songs?" said Polly.

"This time I'll put her in my room and close the door," said Wendy. "Then she can't get out."

After Wendy sat down again, Mortimer began the second tape. "Wait a minute," said Georgie. "I want to get a drink of water."

When he returned, Mortimer looked around at everyone. "Now can we start?"

"Not yet," said Peter. "Look up in the tree." Sure enough, there was Petunia peering down at them from the tree branches.

"Georgie, are you letting Petunia out?" demanded Wendy.

"What are you talking about?" said Georgie.

"Everytime you go in, Petunia gets out," said Wendy.

"That's not my fault," exclaimed Georgie.

"Then how is she getting out of the house?" Wendy asked.

"Well, let's find out," said Georgie. "I have to clear my name."

"Besides," Peter said, "our meeting will never take off until that bird stays put." So the kids set down their sandwiches and

headed for the house. They had a mystery of their own to solve.

First they checked with Mr. White to see if he might have let Petunia out without his knowing. But Mr. White had been outside washing the ground-floor windows for an hour. He hadn't gone inside once.

Then they asked Mrs. White if she opened the door to Wendy's room. "No," she said. "I've been downstairs cleaning the kitchen. I haven't been upstairs at all. I didn't let Petunia out."

"Well, Petunia certainly couldn't open the doors by herself," said Wendy. "Someone is helping her get out."

"We're never going to finish lunch," complained Mortimer. "You should think about getting fish, Wendy. You never have this kind of trouble with them. They never interfere with your lunch schedule."

"Yeah, but fish can't sing," laughed Georgie.

"Let's double-check your room, Wendy," suggested Samantha.

When the kids opened Wendy's door, they found that Petunia was not there.

"Oh, no," cried Peter. "Petunia's outside again!"

"There's no way Petunia could get out with the door closed," said Wendy. "Come on, Georgie, this has to be one of your practical jokes. Did you slip up here again while we were talking to my parents?"

"No joke," said Polly. "I know how Petunia is getting out. And Georgie is in the clear."

**How did Samantha know Georgie wasn't guilty? And how _did_ Petunia get out?**

## Solution
## The Case of the Parrot's Escape

Polly walked over to a window in Wendy's room and swung her fist toward it.

"Watch out!" screamed Wendy. "You'll cut yourself."

"No, I won't," smiled Polly. "The window is open. Your dad must have left it open by mistake after he washed it. No one could tell because he did such a super wash job, you can't see the glass."

The kids went down to get Petunia once more. They told Mr. White what had happened and congratulated him on a wash well done.

"Maybe you'll come over and clean my fish tanks," Mortimer said. "The fish won't know they are behind glass."

"Watch out, Mortimer," replied Mr. White. "They might swim right out of the tank and go up a tree, just like Petunia!"

"Whatever," said Georgie. "At least my name is clear."

"As clear as one of Mr. White's window-panes," laughed Mortimer.

# The Case of the Lost and Found Secret

Early one summer morning, Peter Plum called all the other Clue Club members over to his house. "We've got a case!" he told them. "Come over to my house quick!" Samantha Scarlet and Wendy White were the first to arrive.

"What's going on?" asked Samantha.

"Wait till everyone is here," answered Peter.

Soon Polly Peacock and Mortimer Mustard came running down the block, with Georgie Green riding his bicycle beside them.

"Why did you have to wait for everyone before you could tell us what's going on?" asked Wendy.

"Because it's a little complicated," answered Peter. "June Jade, down the street, called me. She needs our help to solve a robbery."

"What was stolen?" asked Georgie.

"That's just it. I don't know," said Peter.

"You don't know?" said Mortimer. "Why not?"

"IT is a secret," says Peter. "June hid something in a secret place but she won't tell me what it is."

"Then how are we supposed to find it?" asked Georgie. "If we don't know what IT is."

"The only thing June would tell me is she thinks Connie Cardinal took it — whatever IT is," said Peter.

"Connie!" exclaimed Polly. "Connie is June's best friend. Why would June think she took it?"

"First of all, Connie is the only person who knew about IT," said Peter. "Plus Connie knew where IT was hidden. June showed her the hiding spot the day they both left for soccer camp."

"But if they were both away at camp, how could June take it?" asked Wendy.

"I told you this case was complicated," sighed Peter. "Soccer camp was supposed to last a week, but Connie came back a day before June did."

"I get it," interrupted Polly. "Connie could have gone to the hiding place before June got back and then taken the . . . the . . . Oh, whatever it is!"

"Right," said Peter. "But June can't believe Connie would do that. She wants to make sure. That's where we come in."

"So, let me get this straight," said Georgie. "We don't know what's gone, but we're supposed to find out who took it."

"Yep," said Peter. "Sort of, I guess."

The Clue Club looked at each other and shrugged their shoulders.

"I guess the first thing we should do is go over to June's house and look for clues," Wendy said.

The kids walked down the street to

June's house. When they arrived, she was sitting on her porch waiting for them. "Thanks for helping me out," she said. "I don't want to say anything to Connie unless I'm sure she took it."

"Can't you tell us what IT is?" asked Polly. "That might help us find out if she took it."

"I don't really want to say," replied June. "But I'll show you where the hiding place is." She led the kids to the back of her house. At the edge of the backyard was a concrete block wall with flat stones across the top. The wall was almost hidden behind some bushes.

"There's the hiding place," June said, pointing to the wall. "One of the stones on top of the wall is loose. Underneath it is a hole where I put things I want to keep secret. When I came back from camp today, I found the stone on the ground. And the . . . I mean, IT . . . was gone. No one would ever come back here unless they lived here. That's why it had to be Connie.

She was the only one outside of my family who even knows about this wall."

Peter looked around in the grass. "Where's the stone now?" he asked.

"That's funny," June said. "It was right there a little while ago." She pointed to a spot of brown grass by the wall. Then she looked up at the wall and gasped, "Look! Someone put the stone back!" Everyone gathered around June as she lifted a loose stone on top of the wall. "Hey, it's here again!" she yelled out.

"IT! IT! I can't stand it anymore!" Mortimer shouted. "What is IT?"

"I guess I can tell you, now that I have to find another hiding place for it," said June. "IT is my diary."

"Why would Connie want to steal your diary?" asked Polly.

"I can't figure that out, either," answered June. "I tell her all my secrets. I tell her more than I write in my diary. I don't know who would want to read my diary."

"Well, anyway, the diary is back," said Georgie.

"Maybe Connie put it back," said Samantha.

"I don't think so," said Wendy.

"Why not?" asked Samantha.

"Because Connie didn't take it," said Wendy.

"You don't think so?" exclaimed June. "That's a relief. But how can you tell?"

"Because Connie hasn't been back from camp long enough," said Wendy.

**How did Wendy know Connie was innocent?**

Just then someone sneezed in the bushes. It was June's little brother, Patrick.

"What are you doing here, Patrick?" asked June. "Something tells me you did this, you little brat."

"Okay, I took your diary," Patrick said. "But I never read it. It was locked. I looked for the key all week while you were gone but I couldn't find it. I thought you wrote what you got me for my birthday."

"I guess your birthday present, whatever IT is, is still a secret," laughed Georgie.

# Solution
## The Case of the Lost and Found Secret

Wendy pointed to the brown spot in the grass. "The grass under the stone is brown," she said. "That means the area hasn't been getting any sun. But the stone had to be sitting on the grass for more than one day to make it turn brown."

"Can you explain?" asked Georgie.

"Sure," said Wendy. "The diary was in the wall when the girls left for camp. If Connie took it, she would have put the stone on the ground yesterday and then put it back on the wall today. That means the stone would have been on the ground for only one day. That's not enough time for the grass underneath it to turn brown. The stone had to be on the ground for much longer."

"I see," said Peter. "Whoever took the diary, took it right after the girls went away to camp."

# The Case of the Stolen Scene

The fourth grade was putting on a play about a murder that takes place during a masquerade ball. All of the Clue Club members were in the show. Mortimer Mustard had one of the leading roles, as the wealthy businessman who throws the ball. Wendy White played his maid. Peter Plum's character was a professor friend of the businessman. And Polly Peacock, Samantha Scarlet, and Georgie Green were guests at the ball.

Mortimer loved being in the play and being onstage. But he was still upset about not getting the role of the detective who solves the murder. That part went to Rodney Redbrush. Mortimer was still complaining about Rodney during the final dress rehearsal.

"Why didn't I get that role?" he complained to the others during a break. "Rodney doesn't know what a detective does. I've studied how to be a detective by playing Clue Jr. for hours. Not to mention all the mystery books I've read and movies I've watched. It's just not fair."

"Oh, get over it," said Polly. "Opening night is tomorrow and you're still moaning over your part."

"You should quit complaining about Rodney and watch your own character," said Wendy. "You're always upstaging everyone."

"Yeah," said Tommy Topaz. He was a guest at the ball in the last scene. "That's not good acting. That's good hogging."

"Let's go through the final scene, kids," said Ms. Brightman, the drama teacher. "Then we'll go home."

The final scene took place during the ball. Rodney was about to reveal who the murderer was when Mortimer walked in front of him. Rodney threw up his hands.

"He keeps walking in front of me," Rodney complained to Ms. Brightman. "I'm the one who figures out who the murderer is, not Mortimer. Why does he always try to steal this scene?"

Ms. Brightman sighed and gave Mortimer his stage directions once more. "Now, Mortimer, we've gone over this before. Rodney is the character with the important lines in this scene. You walk behind him, not in front of him. Try to remember that."

Then she turned to the rest of the cast. "All right, boys and girls, that's it for tonight. Be here tomorrow at six o'clock sharp. And what is tomorrow?"

"OPENING NIGHT!" the kids shouted. Then they gave a cheer and ran to the dressing rooms to change and go home. As they were leaving the school, Rodney ran up to Mortimer. "I've had it with you, you spoiled brat," he said to Mortimer. "You're just mad because Ms. Brightman thought I'd make a better detective than you. But you don't have to ruin my performance.

Don't walk in front of me again, do you hear?" Rodney was so mad, he was yelling at the top of his lungs.

"Fine! You don't have to get so mad," said Mortimer.

"Well, you can't blame him," said Samantha. "I'd be angry, too."

Rodney didn't scare Mortimer. Mortimer was so excited about being in the play, he was the first one to arrive at the school for the opening night performance. Mortimer was always the first one at rehearsals, but tonight Rodney was already in the dressing room. He was dressed in a cape, long wig, and big feathered hat. It was the pirate costume that Rodney's detective character wears to the ball.

"Hey, Rodney, you're here early," Mortimer said. Rodney was standing with his back to Mortimer and didn't turn around or say a word. *I guess he's still so mad he won't speak to me*, Mortimer thought to himself.

"Is Ms. Brightman helping you with

your lines?" Mortimer said, trying to aggravate Rodney. Rodney shook his head.

Mortimer kept up the teasing. "Don't forget to change your shoes before the show," he said. "Remember, you don't wear sneakers, you wear boots." Rodney only nodded.

"He's so mad he won't even look at me," Mortimer decided. He walked to the costume room to get his costume and when he returned, Rodney was gone. "I guess he can't even stand to be in the same room with me," Mortimer chuckled. "You'd think he could be a little nicer."

Soon Peter and Polly came in carrying their costumes. Then Georgie, Samantha, and Wendy came through the door already dressed.

"Well, everyone," said Wendy. "Break a leg! Only not for real, of course."

"I see you're the first one here again, Mortimer," laughed Polly.

"Don't worry, Mortimer," said Peter.

"No one will steal your character if you're late."

"I wasn't the first one here tonight. So there," Mortimer told them. "Rodney was here first, already dressed in his costume. He is mad, too. Won't speak or even look at me."

"Can't blame him, Mortimer," said Peter. "Try not to grab the spotlight tonight."

Almost everyone in the cast was there. Rodney walked into the dressing room. He was in costume except for his sneakers. Mortimer called out to him, "Don't forget you still have to change into your pirate boots."

"I just got here, Mustard," Rodney snapped, "and already you're telling me what to do."

Just then Mary Amber, the cook in the play, jumped up from a dressing table. "My Walkman is gone," she yelled. "I left it here yesterday after rehearsal."

"I remember seeing it when I came in around five o'clock today," Ms. Brightman said. "Mortimer, you were the first one here. Did you see the Walkman?"

"I don't remember whether it was here or not," said Mortimer. "But I wasn't the first one here tonight. Rodney was. Maybe he saw it."

"Yes, Rodney was the first one here tonight," Tommy Topaz piped up.

"Maybe Rodney took it," said Amber.

"What's going on?" cried Rodney. "I just got here a few minutes ago."

"No," said Mortimer. "You were in the dressing room when I came in. Then you left. I figured you were so mad at me you didn't want to be in the same room."

"You're nuts, Mortimer," yelled Rodney. "I just got here. You're always the first one here. I'll bet you're the one."

"Well, Mortimer, you were the first one I saw this evening," admitted Ms. Brightman.

"First he tries to steal my scene, then

he steals Mary's Walkman," shouted Rodney. "And he's trying to frame me for it so I'll get kicked out of the play. Then you could be the detective. Right, Mustard?"

"Come on, Clue Club, let's show Rodney how a real detective solves a crime," sniffed Mortimer. "Let's look at the clues."

Peter began to walk back and forth. "Rodney," he said, "do you have any black sneakers?"

"No," answered Rodney.

Peter pointed to Rodney's sneakers. "Mortimer, remember you said Rodney was wearing black sneakers when you first saw him in the dressing room?" he said. Mortimer nodded.

"Come to think of it, I never saw Rodney's face," Mortimer said. "I only saw the back of Rodney's costume and the black sneakers."

"Anyone could have put on Rodney's costume and pretended to be him," said Wendy.

"I agree that this scene is a frame-up,"

Peter said. "But Mortimer's not the one who set the stage."

"I know who walked away with the Walkman," declared Polly.

**Who took the Walkman?**
**And how does Polly know?**

man. "Luckily, your role had no lines and someone else can fill in easily."

"So the show will go on," cheered Georgie.

"I'm glad this scene wasn't a showstopper," said Mortimer.

# Solution
## The Case of the Stolen Scene

Polly pointed to Tommy Topaz. "What color sneakers is Tommy wearing?" she asked.

"That doesn't prove anything," Tommy protested. "Lots of kids have black sneakers."

"Then how did you know that Rodney was the first one to arrive?" said Polly.

Georgie answered Polly's question for Tommy. "Because he was already here."

"Dressed up in Rodney's costume," said Wendy.

"All right," Tommy said. "I came early to take the Walkman. When I heard Mortimer come in, I put on Rodney's costume to hide myself and make it look like Rodney took the Walkman. I guess that means I'm out of the play."

"I'm afraid so, Tommy," said Ms. Bright-

# The Case of the Missing Link

It was Friday. And it was the last period of the school day. In twenty minutes the weekend would begin. Ms. Redding stepped in front of her fourth-grade class. "Students, I have a surprise for you," she said. "As you know, the Hobart Art Museum is opening its new dinosaur room next week. Scientists have been putting a dinosaur skeleton together for nearly a year. Today I spoke with Mr. Greenfield, the head of the museum. He's agreed to let you watch them finish the project tomorrow morning."

The six members of the Clue Club looked at each other. They usually had their club meetings on Saturday mornings. They hated to miss one — even to see the new dinosaur exhibit.

"Now, class, can anyone tell me what a paleontologist is?" Ms. Redding asked.

Wendy White raised her hand.

"Yes, Wendy," said Ms. Redding.

"Isn't that a scientist who looks for dinosaur bones?" answered Wendy.

"That's right," replied Ms. Redding. "Paleontologists look for ancient bones and other kinds of fossils. Studying these fossils helps them learn about creatures and plants that lived long ago."

Georgie Green's hand shot up. But before Ms. Redding could call on him, he blurted out, "So dinosaur bones are like clues?"

"Yes, Georgie," said Ms. Redding, smiling. "Bones are clues that tell paleontologists what dinosaurs looked like, what they ate, and how they lived."

Ms. Redding told the class they had to be at the museum by eight-thirty. Mr. Greenfield wanted the students to finish their tour before the museum opened at ten A.M. "The side door will be left open for you," she told the class.

Just then the bell rang. Everyone grabbed their backpacks and ran for the door. "See you tomorrow, class," called Ms. Redding.

The Clue Club gathered together on the playground.

"Let's have our Clue Club meeting after we go to the museum tomorrow," said Mortimer Mustard.

All the members agreed.

"We might even find a mystery to solve at the museum!" Polly Peacock said.

"Like the paleontologists. They must love mysteries, too," said Georgie. "What happened to dinosaurs is one of the neatest mysteries in the world!"

"Why don't we ride our bikes?" said Samantha Scarlet. "We can take the road across Hobart Bridge."

The kids decided to meet at Peter Plum's house since it was closest to the bridge. Everyone was excited about the trip.

The next morning Peter woke up with a wet face. His dog, Bizzy, was licking him. Just then Peter heard a loud *Brrrrring! Brrrrring!* It was the doorbell. He grabbed his glasses and looked at his clock. "Holy cow! My alarm didn't go off!" Peter threw back the covers. "Just a minute!" he shouted. "I'm coming!"

The whole Clue Club was standing at Peter's front door. "I overslept," he shrugged.

"I don't believe it, Peter!" exclaimed Polly. "You're not even dressed." She rolled her eyes.

"I'm sorry," he stammered. "I was up late last night reading."

"You were reading?" laughed Mortimer. "So what else is new, Peter?" Everyone else laughed. Peter was a well-known bookworm.

Peter yawned, wiping the sleep from his eyes. "But I was reading about dinosaur bones — " he began.

Samantha interrupted him. "Well, if you don't hurry up, we'll miss our chance to see one being put together."

"Can we help you get ready, Peter?" asked Wendy.

"Ahh, yeah," answered Peter. "My mom and dad must have gone to the store. I'm supposed to walk Bizzy and put him on his leash in the backyard."

"I'll take care of that while you get dressed," said Georgie.

Peter pulled on his jeans and a T-shirt. He grabbed a doughnut, ran outside, and bumped his bike down his front porch stairs. "Okay, I'm ready," he shouted. "Where's Bizzy?"

"He's fine," called Georgie. "I walked him and put him on his leash. Let's go!"

"I'd better make sure," said Peter. He knew Georgie sometimes did things in a hurry. "Mom and Dad will be real mad if he gets loose."

"Nah," laughed Georgie. "He's fine! Come on, you'll make us late!"

"Well," said Peter, "I sure don't want to miss anything. Let's go!" he shouted.

The town of Hobart was just on the other side of the bridge. So it didn't take the bikers long to reach the museum. When they entered the side door, Mr. Greenfield was sitting in his office right across the hall. He got up and waved to them. "Just in time," he smiled. "The rest of the class is already upstairs. Come on. I think you'll enjoy this!"

Mr. Greenfield led them upstairs to a large room with a high ceiling. In the center, the dinosaur skeleton stood on a low platform. On the floor around the dinosaur, some of the workers were laying out the dinosaur's leg and foot bones.

"Gee," Peter said to Georgie, "some of these small bones look just like the plastic ones Bizzy chews on for his teeth."

Other workers were wiring the bones together. One of them walked over to the group.

"Class, this is Dr. Eagle," announced

Mr. Greenfield. "Dr. Eagle is a paleontologist. He's in charge of putting the dinosaur skeleton together."

"Hello, kids," said Dr. Eagle. "Do any of you know how we get the dinosaur to a museum after we find it?"

Peter stepped forward. "I do," he said. "I did some reading last night."

"Ohhh," Polly moaned.

"Why don't you tell us what you read," said Dr. Eagle.

Peter straightened his glasses. "Well," he began, "after a bone is found, it's cleaned. Then plaster is poured around it. The hard plaster keeps the bone from getting broken when it's shipped to the museum. It's sort of like when you break your arm and you get a plaster cast on it. The cast protects the bone. When the bones reach the museum, the plaster gets chipped off. Then the bones are wired together."

Peter looked up at Dr. Eagle. "Right?" he asked.

"Right!" exclaimed Dr. Eagle, smiling. "We've been removing the plaster in a room across the hall. Then we lay the bones out in here before we wire them together. Let's go take a look at the ones we're working with now." And he began walking to the other side of the room.

Just then Peter saw Samantha waving to him from the hall. Everyone was following Dr. Eagle so no one noticed Peter slip out the door.

"Look who's here!" whispered Samantha. Peter looked down. Samantha was holding Bizzy by the collar.

"Bizzy!" exclaimed Peter.

"Shhhh!" said Samantha. "Yes, Bizzy! I went to get a drink. That's when I heard him barking in the room across the hall. He was scratching through a pile of paper and plaster next to that big trash bin. You're lucky no one else heard him."

"I knew I should have checked his leash," groaned Peter. "He must have gotten loose and followed us."

"Yeah, it's no mystery what happened," agreed Samantha. "But now what?"

"I don't want to miss what Dr. Eagle is saying," said Peter. "We'll have to sneak Bizzy in." He looked down at his dog and said sternly, "Now, you keep still, Bizzy."

Peter waited outside the dinosaur room holding Bizzy. Meanwhile, Samantha told the other club members what happened. They tried to keep Bizzy hidden by standing in a circle around him. But as soon as Bizzy saw the dinosaur inside the exhibit room, he got very excited. He ran through everyone's legs and started barking at the huge skeleton.

For a second, Mr. Greenfield and Dr. Eagle just looked at Bizzy with their mouths open. Then they both dived for the dog. But Bizzy promptly zipped out of the room and down the stairs.

Mr. Greenfield sat up on the floor. "How did that dog get in here?" he sputtered.

"He followed me from home," said Peter meekly.

"Well, CATCH HIM THIS INSTANT!" shouted Mr. Greenfield.

"And don't let him touch any dinosaur bones!" yelled Dr. Eagle.

Bizzy thought this was a wonderful game of chase. He ran around the fountain in the museum lobby then back up the stairs. Then he ran around the dinosaur a couple of times before the kids trapped him in the room across the hall near the trash bin.

"Now, take your dog outside," ordered Mr. Greenfield. Peter hung his head.

"I'm glad I have a turtle for a pet," Polly said to Peter as he carried Bizzy out the door.

Outside, Peter tied his dog to the bike rack. "Now you've gotten us in trouble," he sighed.

But back inside the museum, there was more trouble for Peter. Mr. Greenfield was standing with his hands on his hips, waiting for him. "It looks like your dog made off with some bones, after all," he said. "Three

70

are missing and they were all here yesterday when we cleaned them."

"But that can't be!" said Peter. "We
would have seen him take the bones."

Then he remembered! "No," Peter
cried, "Bizzy didn't take the bones, but I'll
bet he can help us find them!"

**What happened to the bones?
And how could Bizzy help Peter find
them?**

"If it weren't for Bizzy," said Mr. Green-field, "we might have thrown out these priceless bones."

"Looks like Bizzy is a kind of paleontol-ogist, too," laughed Dr. Eagle. "It seems he's pretty good at finding dinosaur bones."

# Solution
# The Case of the Missing Link

"Oh, no you don't," said Mr. Greenfield. "That dog's not coming in here again."

"It's all right, Mr. Greenfield," said Peter. "Bizzy's already found the bones. Right, Samantha?" Peter pointed to a pile of paper and plaster near the trash bin.

"Oh, yeah! I get it!" exclaimed Samantha. "When I first found Bizzy, he was scratching near that trash bin."

"Maybe we should see what he was looking for," said Peter.

So Dr. Eagle and a couple of the workers carefully checked through the pile of plaster. Sure enough, there was a dinosaur bone mixed up in the garbage. "Bizzy probably thought it was one of his plastic teething bones," Peter said.

"We'd better look through the trash bin, too," said Dr. Eagle. Soon the workers found the other missing bones. They had been put into the trash by accident.

# The Case that Snowballed

*B*rrrrinnng! Samantha Scarlet yawned and looked at her alarm clock. Seven o'clock. Time to get up for school. Last night, before she went to sleep, the weather report predicted a snowstorm. She got out of bed and looked out her bedroom window. "Please, please, please," she said. Sure enough, her yard and the street were blanketed with snow!

"Yes!" Samantha exclaimed, jumping up and down. "It's at least a foot!"

Just then her mother called up the stairs. "No school today, Samantha."

"Yesss!" Samantha yelled. She picked up the phone to call the other Clue Club members. She dialed Wendy White first. Wendy was her best friend.

"No school today, Wendy. Let's rent a mystery movie," said Samantha.

"Fine with me," said Wendy. "Let's call the rest of the Clue Club."

So Samantha called Georgie Green, then Peter Plum, and then Polly Peacock. Everyone thought curling up with a movie was a great idea for a cold day. Finally, Samantha called Mortimer Mustard.

"Since there's no school today, everyone wants to rent a mystery movie," Samantha said. "You want to?"

"Yeah, but I think we should go sledding on Slippery Slope first," Mortimer answered. "I have a new toboggan I want to try out. And it's big enough for at least three kids!"

"Wow! That sounds great!" exclaimed Samantha. "We can watch the movie afterward. Let's call the others."

"Right," said Mortimer. "Meet at my house."

Within half an hour, the Clue Club gang

was in front of Mortimer's house with their sleds.

"Looks like Jimmy and Jeff Black are making a snowman," said Wendy. She pointed to the two brothers who lived next door to Mortimer. The boys were rolling a big ball of snow in the yard next to the Mustards' garage.

"Jimmy sure is rolling a huge snowball," said Samantha. "That snowman's going to be one tall dude."

"A snowman," said Mortimer. "How childish of them."

"Ah, Mortimer," sighed Georgie. "How oldish of you."

Everyone reminded Mortimer about the fantastic snow sculpture he made a few weeks ago during the last snowstorm.

"Yes, but that was art," explained Mortimer. "I was trying to create a —"

"Okay, okay, Mortimer Michelangelo," sniffed Polly.

"Actually, today's snow is perfect for

sculpting," said Mortimer, "but I think I'd rather try out my new toboggan."

"You have a toboggan?" Georgie asked. "That's great. We could all go down the hill together in a toboggan."

"Speaking of your new toboggan, let's see it, Mortimer," said Peter.

"It's in the garage," said Mortimer, opening the garage door.

Inside, the kids examined the toboggan. "I'll bet four of us can fit on this, Mortimer," said Polly excitedly. "It's great!"

"Wait," Mortimer went on. "There's more. Check these out!" He pointed to a box labeled IGLOO ICE SKATES sitting on a high shelf in the garage.

"Wow, Mortimer!" gasped Peter. "Igloos are the best skates!"

"Yeah, I know," said Mortimer proudly. "My parents probably wanted to surprise me. They put them up there thinking I wouldn't be able to see them. But, of course, I spotted the box right away. I'll

bet they didn't want to give me the toboggan and the skates at one time."

"Well, we're happy you got your toboggan, Mortimer," said Polly. "Come on, let's
hit the slope."

The kids pulled their sleds to the park.
Just past the lake inside the park was Slippery Slope.

"Everyone from school is here," yelled
Peter.

"Look, the lake is frozen," exclaimed
Wendy. "Some kids are skating on it."

"Oh, there's Jimmy Black. I didn't know
he had ice skates," said Mortimer. "Hey,
Jimmy!" he shouted, but Jimmy skated
away.

"Maybe he didn't hear you. He's too far
away," said Peter. "Who goes first on the
toboggan?"

"I do, of course," declared Mortimer.

For the next couple of hours, the kids
sledded down the hill, walked back up, and
sledded down again. Finally, Mortimer

shouted to his friends, "I'm freezing! Let's go have hot chocolate at my house."

"Now that's a warm thought," yelled Peter. They gathered up their sleds and trooped back to Mortimer's house. In front of the garage they stomped and brushed the snow off their boots and coats.

"Looks like Jimmy and Jeff never finished their giant snowman," said Wendy. "They only made the two small snowballs."

Mortimer lifted the garage door to put up his toboggan.

"Umm," sighed Wendy, "nice and warm in here."

"Yeah, Dad's sports car doesn't run too well in the cold," laughed Mortimer. "Hey!" he yelled, looking up. "My skates! They're gone!"

"Maybe your parents decided you had enough toys after all," said Polly, kidding Mortimer.

"Or maybe they moved them," said Mortimer. "I'll go check."

Mortimer ran inside his house. A few minutes later, he came back with a long face.

"No, they didn't move the skates," he said. "And they're in a bad mood because I found them." Then his face brightened. "But at least they didn't take them back to the store."

"Let's take a look around," said Peter. "Maybe we'll find some clues to this mystery." Everyone gathered under the shelf and looked up at it.

"That shelf is high up," said Samantha. "How did the thief get the skates down from there?"

"Good question," said Wendy. "There's nothing in here to climb on, not even a table or bench."

"Yeah," said Mortimer. "Dad keeps all the ladders and tool stuff locked in the toolshed."

"Someone could have brought in a ladder," said Peter. "Let's check the snow for tracks."

The kids looked around outside in the snow for tracks. "Nobody dragged a ladder or table into the garage," said Samantha.

"Wait," said Georgie. "I'm warming up to this case. I'll bet I know who did it and what was used to get the skates down. Our problem is that the main clue is missing."

"What happened to it?" asked Peter.

**Do you know who took the skates and how? And what *is* the missing clue?**

## Solution
## The Case that Snowballed

"The main clue melted," said Georgie. "Remember the huge snowball Jimmy and Jeff were rolling this morning? It's gone. I think Jimmy rolled the snowball into the garage and stood on it to reach the skates. Then he went to the lake to skate. The snowball melted inside the warm garage."

"All that's left of it is that big puddle of water on the floor of the garage," Peter said.

"And remember when we saw Jimmy ice-skating at the lake?" asked Georgie. "You said he didn't have any ice skates."

"That's right," said Wendy. "Maybe that's why he ignored you when you called to him."

"I think so, too," said Georgie.

"There's only one thing to do," said Mortimer. "Let's go to Jimmy's house."

As soon as the kids presented their clues, Jimmy confessed. "I was jealous of all the things you have," he told Mortimer. "I was going to put the skates back tonight, I swear."

"That's a lousy thing to do to your next-door neighbor," said Mortimer. "I didn't even get to wear the skates first."

"That was a pretty cool ladder, Jimmy, but thanks to Georgie's hot detective work, your scheme was a meltdown," Samantha laughed.

"There's one good thing," said Mortimer. "My parents will probably let me have the skates now. I won't have to wait."

"Then what are we waiting for?" said Wendy. "Let's go skating!"